Fowl Mouthwash

Real heroes read!

Smith Road Elementary
Media Center
1135 Smith Road
Temperance, MI 48182

This book is fiction. The people, places, events, and cluck-o-bots depicted within are fictitious. Any resemblance to persons living or dead or to real life places is purely coincidence and, in all honesty, probably a little disturbing.

No part of this publication may be reproduced in whole or in part, or stored in a retrieval system, or transmitted in any form or by any means, electronic, mechanical, photocopying, recording, or otherwise, without written permission of the publisher. For information regarding permission, write to Sigil Publishing, Box 824, Leland, Michigan 49654.

ISBN 978-0-9785642-3-5

Copyright © 2008 by Sigil Publishing. All rights reserved. Heroes A2Z is copyright © 2007, Sigil Publishing.

Printed in the U.S.A.

First Printing, October 2008

Don't Play Chicken With These Birds ...

Cock-a-Doodle-DOOM!

CONTENTS

1. Meet the Heroes......................................9
2. Cock-a-Doodle-Doom!..........................14
3. Cluck-Cluck...20
4. Sold Out..25
5. Chicken Fever..29
6. Duncan McDoughnut...............................33
7. Cuckoo Cops...38
8. Snowmocycle..44
9. Cluck-o-bot Crossfire..............................51
10. Speak Like Chickens..............................56

11. Welcome to Frankencoop........................63
12. The Real Henry Cooper.........................70
13. Hero Hurricane.................................77
14. Eggsitting.....................................83
15. Frankenbeak and Hoofenstein..................89
16. Playing Chicken................................93
17. Rooster-Go-Round..............................98
18. Bark Then Bwack..............................104
19. Horn of Heroes...............................110

Real Heroes Read!
realheroesread.com

#6: Fowl Mouthwash

David Anthony
and
Charles David

Illustrations
Lys Blakeslee

Traverse City, MI

Home of the Heroes

abigail

andrew

zoë

CHAPTER 1: MEET THE HEROES

Welcome to Traverse City, Michigan, population 18,000. The city has everything you might expect: malls, movie theaters, schools, and playgrounds. Kids swim here in the summer and build snowmen during the winter. Sometimes they pretend that they live in an ordinary place.

But Traverse City is far from ordinary. It is set on one of the Great Lakes and attracts tourists in every season. Thousands of people visit every year.

Still, few of them know the city's real secret. Even fewer talk about it. You see, Traverse City is home to three fantastic superheroes. This story is about them.

Meet Abigail, the oldest of our heroes by a whole eight minutes. When it comes to sports, she can't be beat—not at fencing, not at football, and certainly not at field hockey. In the winter she's comfortable on skates, skis, and snowboards. Abominable Snowman beware!

Andrew comes next. He's Abigail's twin brother, younger by a measly eight minutes. If it has wheels, Andrew can ride it. He's fast, fearless, and formidable on wheels. In fact, no one keeps the streets of Traverse City cleaner after a heavy snowfall.

Last but definitely not least is Baby Zoë. She's proof that big things can come in small packages. She still wears a diaper, but she isn't afraid to square off against a 1,000-pound polar bear in the sumo ring. She puts the *pro* in *protection*.

Together these three heroes keep the streets and neighborhoods of Traverse City, Michigan, and America safe. Together they are …

CHAPTER 2:
COCK-A-DOODLE-DOOM!

"Fever," Zoë said, her hand pressed against Mom's forehead.

She and her siblings were hunched over their parents, trying not to look worried. Below them, Mom and Dad lay shivering in bed. The pair had the covers pulled up to their chins and thermometers sticking out of their mouths. They had caught the cold that was going around this winter.

"Is it *starve a cold, feed a fever*?" Abigail wondered. "Or is it the other way around? I can never remember."

Andrew nudged her in the ribs playfully. "I'm pretty sure it's *starve the sisters, feed the brother*," he joked. "Especially at dessert."

Mom ended the debate. "Chicken soup," she requested.

"With crackers," Dad added.

"Your wish is our command," Abigail said with a bow.

"Forthright," Zoë saluted, meaning the heroes would put on their aprons and get cooking immediately.

Downstairs they sped and into the kitchen. Abigail scooped up the spoons, Andrew cranked the can opener, and Zoë fanned the flames—all in the blink of an eye.

Or in Zoë's case, *without* the blink of an eye. Because blinking would seriously mess up her aim. She had to have her eyes open to fire her lasers.

As they cooked, the heroes could hear the TV in the living room. The sound was mostly background noise until one commercial caught their attention. A snappy jingle started it off.

Feelin' bad? Feelin' blue?
Got morning breath?
Here's what to do.

Drink some rinse. Drink some soup.
Drink Fowl Mouthwash.
It's good for you.

The commercial was for chicken soup mouthwash. It promised fresh breath and a cure for the common cold all in one. Who'd ever heard of such a thing?

But there it was on the heroes' TV, and they wanted to believe what they saw. Their parents could sure use mouthwash like that now.

Besides, the man in the commercial was dressed in a chicken suit. He flapped his wings, danced, and sang. Even though he was a stranger to the heroes, his silly costume convinced them to trust him.

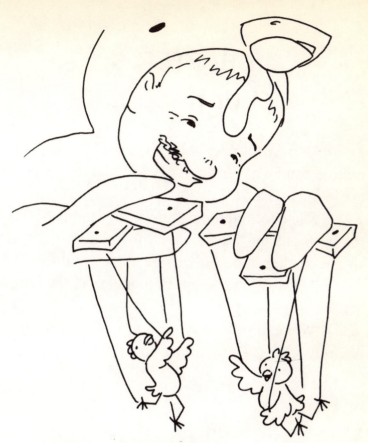

Which was exactly what the man in the chicken suit wanted. His name was Henry Cooper, and he wanted viewers to trust him. He wanted them to believe.

Every time he sang his jingle, he was thinking, "Buy my mouthwash. Drink it, drink it. Say so long to bad breath. Say goodbye to colds. Just keep drinking until my mouthwash is all gone. Then you will be under my control."

Cock-a-doodle-DOOM!

CHAPTER 3: CLUCK-CLUCK

"Uh oh, fumble," Abigail said when the chicken noodle soup was ready. "We don't have any crackers in the house."

She checked the cabinets, the cupboards, and the cushions on the couch. But she didn't corral a single cracker. She only came across crumbs.

"Funds," Zoë suggested, meaning the heroes needed to go shopping.

"We can buy some of that mouthwash, too," Andrew said. "The kind we saw on TV."

Zoë zoomed the soup upstairs to Mom and Dad, and then met her siblings outside. Luckily she could fly. Otherwise she would have had trouble spotting Abigail and Andrew. The snow was almost as deep as she was tall!

Traverse City was known worldwide for cherries, but its average snowfall was over eighty inches a year. That's about seven feet! Try baking a pie out of that.

People up and down the street were outside enjoying the winter weather. Some were having snowball fights. Others were building forts and snowmen.

One pair, however, was building something unusual. The heroes' friends Princess and Rabbit were building a giant snow-chicken!

"Hi, Rabbit," Abigail waved.

"Hey, Princess," Andrew called.

"*Cluck-cluck*," Rabbit and Princess said, too busy for chitchat. How odd!

The day got odder when they reached the market. A group of townsfolk was clapping and flapping their arms to the chicken dance in the parking lot. That silly dance was usually performed only at weddings and baseball games. The heroes had never seen it danced anywhere else, and certainly not outside in the snow.

Inside the market, the odd sights became plain weird. Several townsfolk had removed all of the egg cartons from the dairy cooler and had stacked them on the floor. Even weirder, the people were sitting on the cartons like hens in a chicken coop.

"What's going on here?" Abigail asked the townsfolk. Building snow-chickens and dancing were normal kinds of strange. Sitting on egg cartons like mother hens was a crazy kind of weird.

"*Cluck-cluck*," the townsfolk responded.

The heroes were beginning to think that everyone in town had gone mad. Had Traverse City gone to the birds?

CHAPTER 4:
SOLD OUT

"Cruise over here and check this out," Andrew called to his sisters.

He was across the store and looking at a sold-out display. Next to him stood a life-size cardboard stand-up poster of Henry Cooper, the man in the chicken suit. The nearby shelves were completely empty.

"Someone bought up all the Fowl Mouthwash," Abigail observed.

"Not someone," Mr. Wally Markets, the storeowner, said. "Two someones. A pair of kids about your age bought every bottle I had. Funny thing, one was dressed like a queen. The other one a beaver."

A queen and a beaver! Hearing that, the heroes couldn't help thinking of Princess and Rabbit. A queen was too much like a princess, and a beaver's teeth were too much like a rabbit's. Princess and Rabbit had be the ones who had bought all the mouthwash.

"We'll take these," Abigail said, holding up a box of crackers and handing Mr. Markets some money. "Keep the change."

"And thanks for the information," Andrew added as the heroes dashed out the door.

The trio arrived back home just in time to see Princess and Rabbit walking down their driveway. Rabbit was pulling an empty sled behind him.

"Um, hi, guys," Abigail said, surprised to see their friends at her house.

Andrew got right to the point. "What did you do with all that mouthwash?" he demanded.

But Princess and Rabbit didn't even glance at the heroes. "*Cluck-cluck*," they said, walking right on by.

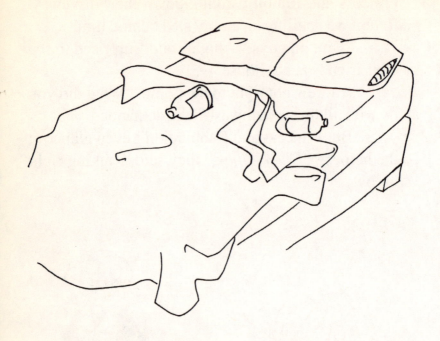

"Something strange is going on," Abigail muttered.

"Fishy," agreed Zoë.

"Let's check on Mom and Dad," Andrew said.

So inside the house and back upstairs the heroes hurried. What they discovered there was worse than they had imagined.

Mom and Dad were not in bed. They were gone. Missing! The only clue to their whereabouts was two empty bottles of Fowl Mouthwash lying on the mattress.

CHAPTER 5: CHICKEN FEVER

Cluck-cluck. Cluck-cluck.

Zoë cocked her head. "Flock?" she asked the twins.

Sure enough, Andrew and Abigail heard it, too. A loud cluck-clucking was coming from the backyard.

"Did Princess and Rabbit come back?" Andrew wondered.

"Maybe someone followed us home from the store?" Abigail suggested.

The heroes rushed into the backyard. They froze at what they saw there. No one had followed them home. Princess and Rabbit hadn't returned.

The clucking was coming from Mom and Dad. The pair was pecking and scratching the snowy ground like hungry chickens in a barnyard.

Cluck-cluck.

"Mom!" Abigail gasped.

"Dad!" Andrew exclaimed.

"Family!" Zoë gawked. Both parents were behaving like chickens.

Maybe you've heard of the bird flu. Well, Mom and Dad had it worse. They were suffering from a severe case of chicken fever. Something had to be done!

No amount of pinching, poking, pleading, or prodding could cure Mom and Dad of their sickness either. The heroes tried everything, but they couldn't snap their parents out of it.

Finally they gave up and went inside. Mom and Dad continued to cluck and peck in the snow.

"Should we call a doctor?" Abigail asked. Then she shrugged. "Maybe a veterinarian."

Zoë shook her head. "Fraternal," she said, as in the fraternal order of police. Zoë wanted to go to the cops. It wasn't just their parents acting like chickens. Almost everyone in Traverse City had flown the coop.

CHAPTER 6:
DUNCAN McDOUGHNUT

"I think Zoë is right," Andrew said. "We should go to the police."

Of course that was what they should do. Not every town was as lucky as Traverse City. Most didn't have their very own team of superheroes. The next best thing, then, was the police. Its men and women were every bit as brave and helpful as the heroes.

Besides, if the average person looked up to the heroes, who did the heroes look up to? Not themselves! They admired the police. To the heroes, there were no better role models.

The Traverse City police station was south of downtown on a wooded hill. The heroes arrived in minutes, barely out of breath. Flying, running, and cycling—which is exactly how they traveled—never wore them out.

Think of the heroes as fish. Do fish ever get tired of swimming? Of course not. It's what they do and who they are. The same goes for Zoë's flying, Abigail's running, and Andrew's cycling.

The heroes' favorite officer, Sergeant Duncan McDoughnut, met them at the front desk. He sneezed loudly into a handkerchief as the trio approached.

"Forceful," Zoë marveled. She was afraid the officer would blow his mustache off with another blast like that.

Sergeant McDoughnut frowned. "Pardon me," he apologized quickly. "I seem to have *cluck*-caught whatever is going around."

When the heroes heard the sergeant speak, they froze like they had in their backyard. Cluck, the officer had said, just like their parents.

"Would you repeat that?" Abigail asked, trying to sound calm. But her stomach was anything but calm. It was doing loop-de-loops.

The officer shrugged. "Big deal, I sneezed," he said, forcing a smile. "It's nothing to worry about. I have a little *cluck*-cold, that's all."

Andrew had heard enough. The officer had clucked two times too many. "Floor it!" he yelled. "Officer McDoughnut is one of them. He's got chicken fever."

Andrew's warning came just in time. Because Officer McDoughnut was on his feet and reaching for something in his desk.

"Firearm!" Zoë shrieked, expecting to see a gun.

But the officer pulled something else from the drawer. It was a plastic bottle shaped like a chicken and full of green liquid. It was Fowl Mouthwash.

"*Cluck*-come here," Officer Duncan McDoughnut snarled. "It's time for you to take your medicine."

CHAPTER 7: CUCKOO COPS

"It's the mouthwash!" Abigail exclaimed. "That's what's making everyone act like chickens."

"Formula," Zoë said darkly, her eyes narrowing.

Fowl Mouthwash wasn't what the man on TV claimed it to be. The commercial was a lie. The mouthwash didn't cure colds or bad breath. It made people think they were chickens.

Andrew grabbed his sisters by their elbows. "Good job, detectives," he said. "But we still have to get out of here. Now step on it!"

At that moment, it didn't matter that the mouthwash was some kind of diabolic secret formula. What mattered was that Officer McDoughnut and the rest of the cops in the station were clucking madly and charging toward the heroes. All of them clutched bottles of mouthwash in their fists.

"*Cluck*-capture them!" the sergeant shouted.

Without another word, the heroes sped out the front doors and into bigger trouble. Sirens blared to their right and left. Two police cruisers squealed to a stop in front of the station. Clucking cops scrambled out of the cars, and an angry voice shouted at the heroes over a loudspeaker.

"This is the *cluck*-cops," it said. "You're under arrest. Put your hands in the air."

"Look out!" Andrew yelped. "There are more bird-brains up ahead. The whole police force has gone quackers."

Yes, he knew that chickens didn't quack. Ducks did. But the idea was the same. The cops had caught chicken fever from Fowl Mouthwash.

"Quackers!" Abigail cried. "That's it, Andrew. You're brilliant!"

Quickly she reached into her duffle bag and pulled out the box of crackers she had bought at the market. Usually the bag contained only sporting equipment that never weighed her down. That was part of her superpower. But today she was glad she had put the crackers inside.

She tore the box open and scattered them on the ground.

"Feed!" Zoë squealed happily, catching onto her sister's plan. Abigail was trying to distract the cuckoo cops and give the heroes time to escape.

The plan worked, too, exactly as Abigail had hoped. When the cops saw the crackers, they went quackers. They skipped to a stop, bent over at the waist, and started pecking the ground. What had been a hunt for the heroes turned into snacktime at the station.

"Go, go, go!" Abigail roared, shoving her siblings toward the street. "We don't have much time. The crackers won't last forever."

Andrew and Zoë didn't need to be told twice. They turned immediately and raced home. For the moment they were safe. They had escaped the poultry police and were again doing what they did best—flying, running, and wheeling at top speed.

But they weren't completely out of danger yet. Henry Cooper was still out there, hatching his fowl plans and even fouler mouthwash.

CHAPTER 8: SNOWMOCYLCE

Back home, the heroes huddled up like football players in Mom and Dad's room to plan their next move. Being the sports expert, Abigail took charge. She was a natural head coach and leader.

"We need to find the man in the chicken suit," she said. "He's behind this. Henry Cooper. He and his mouthwash."

"Right," said Andrew. "But where do we look?"

A man they had seen on TV could be anywhere—as close as Channel 9 & 10 in Traverse City or as far away as Hollywood, California. The heroes had no idea where the mouthwash commercial had been filmed.

Zoë, however, started searching for clues nearby. She didn't even leave the house. On her parents' bed lay two empty bottles of Fowl Mouthwash. Those told her everything she needed to know.

"Frankenmuth," she said, holding up a bottle for her siblings to read. Printed on the label in all capital letters were the words, "MADE IN FRANKENMUTH, MICHIGAN."

Swack! Smack!

First Andrew slapped his forehead, and then Abigail did the same.

"Frankenmuth!" Andrew exclaimed. "We should have known. Duh!"

Abigail nodded, hand still on her head. "No kidding," she agreed. "Frankenmuth is the chicken capital of Michigan."

She wasn't exaggerating. More than 3 million people visited Frankenmuth, Michigan, every year. They came to shop. They came to visit Bronner's, the world's largest year-round Christmas store. And they came to eat. Homestyle chicken dinners weren't cooked any better than at Zender's Restaurant.

"Frankenmuth is a long way away," Andrew grinned. "So I guess we've got to take a ride. But don't worry. I've got the perfect vehicle. Come on, follow me."

He excitedly led his sisters into the garage and stopped in front of a paint-spattered tarp. Beneath the tarp awaited something his sisters couldn't see. But knowing their brother like they did, they expected it to have wheels.

"Dad and I have been working on this for weeks," Andrew announced proudly. Then he snatched the tarp and threw it aside. "I present my snowmocycle!"

Seeing the snowmocycle caused Abigail to frown. "Is that thing safe?" she asked doubtfully. She had more faith in her tennis shoes and cleats than in the crazy-looking snowmocycle.

"Fast?" Zoë wondered, just hoping for a ride. Like many baby sisters, she didn't doubt her big brother for a moment.

Andrew winked like a used car salesman. "Yep and yep," he said. "It's safe and fast. But probably not in that order."

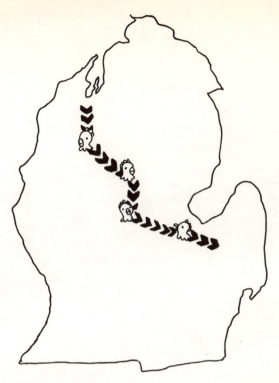

His sisters learned the truth soon. Minutes later they were buckled into the snowmocycle's sidecar and zooming across Michigan alongside their brother.

Crouching low, they headed rapidly southeast, cutting a diagonal snowy path from Traverse City to Frankenmuth. Throughout the journey, they spotted strange behavior in every passing town.

Kids clucked in Clare. Business owners bawked in Buckley. Parents pecked in Mount Pleasant. Seniors scratched in Saginaw. Everywhere the heroes went, people were acting like chickens.

Worst of all was what had become of Frankenmuth, their destination. The heroes had expected to see a cozy, clean city. They had expected buildings that looked like wooden ski lodges high in the mountains.

What they saw caused their hopes to sag. Frankenmuth was no more! The city had become Frankencoop, a fortified fortress for feathered fiends.

CHAPTER 9: CLUCK-O-BOT CROSSFIRE

A tall locked gate was the only way in or out of Frankencoop. Coils of barbed wire and a crooked wall completely surrounded the city.

"Formal?" Zoë suggested, meaning that the heroes shouldn't just smash down the gate. She knew that being polite was usually the best approach. Frankencoop looked uninviting, but that didn't mean the heroes could be rude.

Abigail considered her sister's suggestion and then shrugged. "Why not?" she said. "Let's knock and see who answers."

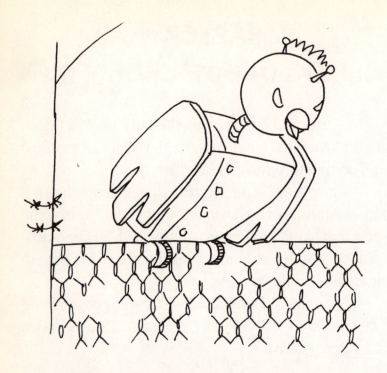

So the heroes started to march toward the forbidding gate. As they did, everything around them went completely still. The only sound was the crunching of their boots in the snow.

Crrrunch! The heroes took one step forward. *Crrrunch!* Then a second. *Crrrunch!* And a third—

"Halt!"

An unexpected voice stopped them in their tracks. On the gate above stood a strange figure. It was half-chicken, half-soldier, and all robot.

"*Cluck*-come no farther," it ordered in a rusty voice.

Andrew raised his arms defensively and took a step back. "We don't want any trouble," he told the chicken-like robot.

Or was it a robot-like chicken? Andrew couldn't tell. So he shrugged and decided to give the creature a new name. He'd call it a cluck-o-bot.

"We just want to speak to the man who makes the mouthwash," Abigail added.

"Friends," Zoë offered with a smile.

Unfortunately the cluck-o-bot didn't believe the heroes. It was a chicken, yes, but it was also a robot. A robot that had been cleverly programmed to keep superheroes out. Henry Cooper didn't like surprise guests.

"Attack!" the cluck-o-bot squawked, flapping its wings like Chicken Little. "Don't let them into our *cluck*-coop!"

Suddenly a dozen more cluck-o-bots appeared on the gate. Six on either side of the first. All of them clutched slingshots loaded with jumbo-sized eggs. All of them took aim at the heroes.

"Attack!" the cluck-o-bot leader squawked again. "Fire!"

Twang! Twang! Twang!

Like trained soldiers, the twelve other cluck-o-bots obeyed. They drew back, they let go, and their slingshots snapped forward. A dozen eggs streaked through the sky. Then a second dozen quickly followed, with another after that.

"Flee!" Zoë shrieked. The cluck-o-bot crossfire was too much. She and her siblings needed to retreat and make a new plan.

CHAPTER 10:
SPEAK LIKE CHICKENS

The heroes' new plan was itchy.

The trio needed to get into Frankenmuth and find Henry Cooper. But they couldn't fight or force their way past the front gate.

So Zoë suggested the only alternative. "Feathers?" she said, and that was the beginning of the mess. Zoë wanted the three superheroes to dress up like chickens!

The problem was they didn't have chicken suits, so they had to wing it—literally. They used the tennis rackets in Abigail's duffel bag for wings. To imitate feathers, they tore open the seat of Andrew's snowmocycle and pulled out the stuffing. For beaks, they clutched crackers between their lips.

"This is never going to work." Abigail muttered.

"What's the matter?" Andrew smirked at her. "Someone ruffle your feathers?"

Abigail just crossed her eyes.

When they approached the gate a second time, the heroes tried to strut like chickens. They bobbed their heads, they flapped their arms, and they paused here and there to peck the ground.

"Halt!" the cluck-o-bot on the gate ordered when it spotted them. "What's the secret password?"

The heroes almost cheered with delight. Their costumes were working. The cluck-o-bot guard thought they were real chickens.

But they still had one more test to pass. One more hurdle to jump before being allowed past the gate.

They had to guess the right password.

Andrew glanced at Abigail. "What do you think the password is?" he whispered without moving his lips.

Abigail shrugged slightly and bent over, pretending to peck for food.

Food! Maybe that was it. The password could be "worms" or "grain" or anything else a chicken might eat. At first Abigail thought she was onto something, but there were still too many choices. Guessing at random would only get her and her siblings caught.

Finally she sighed. "I don't know."

She and Andrew didn't know. But Zoë knew that was because they were thinking too hard. The twins were making it complicated. Abigail and Andrew were trying to guess the cluck-o-bot's password in English. But chickens didn't normally speak English. They spoke chicken.

That meant their secret password would probably be in chicken, too!

"Foreign," Zoë said, as in foreign language. To guess a chicken's password, the heroes needed to think and, more importantly, *speak* like chickens.

Andrew and Abigail stared at each other. Could it be that easy? Could speaking in chicken be all they needed to do?

Like most people, they knew several animal foreign languages. "Moo" meant a lot to cows. "Meow" was a word all cats understood. "Arf," "bark," and "woof" always got a dog's attention.

People were always mooing at cows and barking at dogs. If they didn't expect the animals to understand, why else would they do that?

Among other animal languages, the heroes could speak chicken. They'd been doing so for most of their lives. In fact, nearly everyone in Michigan was speaking chicken today. Their clucking could be heard from Iron Mountain to Ithaca.

Abigail faced the cluck-o-bot on the gate and straightened her shoulders. "*Cluck*," she said, trying to sound confident. Cluck was the one chicken word she knew.

Zoë and Andrew joined her. "*Cluck-cluck*," Andrew said.

Then the heroes waited to see what would happen next.

CHAPTER 11:
WELCOME TO FRANKENCOOP

Feeling very small in front of the gate to Frankencoop, the heroes waited in nervous silence. The cluck-o-bot guard stared down at them hard like a distrustful babysitter. Did it believe their costumes? Had they guessed the right password?

Finally the cluck-o-bot spoke. "You have a strange accent," it declared. "But the password is *cluck*-correct. Welcome to Franken-*cluck*-coop."

Then with the sound of a cracking egg, the gate split in the middle and opened inward. The heroes were being allowed into the city. Their costumes and plan had worked!

As they shuffled through the gate, their mouths—or, like the chickens they were pretending to be, their beaks—fell open. They almost lost their crackers.

The sight of Frankencoop stunned them. Unlike every other town they had seen today, it wasn't full of people acting like chickens. Frankencoop reversed that trend. The city was full of chickens acting like people!

Chickens crowded the schools, shops, sidewalks, and streets. They chatted on cell phones. They hustled to and from appointments. They wore suits and carried briefcases like businesspeople in a big city.

Frankencoop wasn't just a new name, the heroes realized. It was a new way of life for all chickenkind!

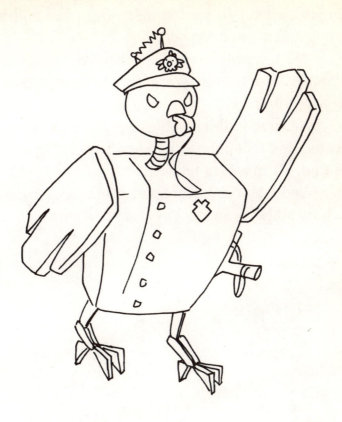

"You there," a rusty voice demanded suddenly. "Why are you just standing around?"

The voice belonged to a burly cluck-o-bot wearing a police officer's uniform. In their shock and surprise, the heroes hadn't noticed the robot approach.

"Um … *cluck-cluck*," Abigail murmured, hoping the chicken language trick would work again.

It didn't. The cluck-o-bot cop didn't fall for Abigail's ruse. It wanted more from her and her siblings. It wanted answers.

"Yes, we all know the password," it said impatiently. "But who are you *cluck*-chickens and what are your jobs?"

No time to think, Abigail responded with the first thought that popped into her head. "Phys Ed," she said. "I'm a gym teacher."

And why not? Her sporty superpower made teaching athletics an ideal job for her.

The cluck-o-bot nodded and turned to Andrew. "And you?" it asked.

"Bus driver," Andrew answered. If his sister could pretend to work at school, so could he. His superpower made it just as likely. Just think how fast he could get the students to class. Hang onto your homework!

Zoë didn't wait to be asked where she worked. As soon as the cluck-o-bot accepted Andrew's answer, she spoke up.

"Faculty," she said, naming another job at school. But she wasn't thinking of just any job. She was thinking principal, the person in charge.

Now if Zoë could only learn to count. "Four, five, fifteen, forty," she mumbled, staring at her fingers bewilderedly. Numbers weren't as easy for her as flying or using x-ray vision. Everyone had their talents.

"*Cluck*-carry on," the cluck-o-bot cop said with authority. "Just be sure to attend this afternoon's meeting. And don't be late." Then it stabbed a wing at a billboard overhead like a person pointing with a thumb.

The heroes glanced up and couldn't believe their luck. First they had tricked their way into town. Then they had conned the cop. Now they were being asked to attend a meeting with the man in the chicken suit.

Things were definitely going their way.

But that was about to change.

CHAPTER 12:
THE REAL HENRY COOPER

Four o'clock couldn't come fast enough for the heroes. Imagine having to wear an itchy chicken costume for hours. It was like Halloween without the candy. All trick and no treat.

"What came first?" Andrew asked, trying to raise his sisters' sagging spirits. "The chicken or the egg?"

Abigail thought for a moment and then smirked. "Neither," she said with phony sweetness. "The older sister always comes first."

"Go soak your tail feathers," Andrew sassed his twin. Abigail was only eight minutes older than he. Even in chicken years, that wasn't long.

"Freeze," Zoë hissed, shushing them both. The meeting was about to begin.

Memorial Park was packed. Rows and rows of chickens stood wing-to-wing, waiting for the man in the chicken suit to arrive. The heroes found a spot in the back and tried not to stand out. In fact, they tried not to stand at all. Even Zoë was taller than the real chickens in attendance.

When Henry Cooper finally appeared, a small girl wearing an egg costume accompanied him. The crowd saw them and went silent. They quit clucking, paused in their pecking, and restrained from rustling their feathers. None of them wanted to miss what Henry Cooper had to say.

"Cock-a-doodle-domination!" he bellowed from a perch atop a picnic table. "Franken-*cluck*-coop is ours!"

Hearing this caused the crowd to go wild. Cuckoo, if you will. They clucked and crowed as if the sun were coming up for the first time.

The man at the center of it all raised his wings, calling for silence. "Cock-a-doodle-double!" he continued. "Michigan is ours. Soon the whole *cluck*-country will be, too!"

That did it. Zoë had seen and heard enough. She leaped into the air, tore off her itchy chicken costume, and pointed at Henry Cooper.

"False!" she howled.

The man wasn't a chicken. He was human and a liar. The crowd needed to know that, and Zoë was about to show them.

Before Abigail or Andrew could stop her, Zoë zoomed forward. Feathers flipped and fluttered in her wake like white waves behind a speedboat. She passed that closely to the heads of the chicken audience.

"Fake!" she growled, repeating her warning.

Then she reached the picnic table, grabbed the man's suit, and yanked.

B-bawk!

The man in the chicken suit squawked one startled squawk. Then his costume came off and his secret identity was revealed.

Henry Cooper was a chicken! A chicken on stilts. The man in the chicken suit had been a chicken in a chicken suit the whole time. What was going on here?

Before the heroes could figure it out, the small girl in the egg costume leaped onto the picnic table.

"Stop them!" she cried. "Capture them! Don't let them escape!"

Twelve cluck-o-bots marched forward and saluted.

"*Cluck-cluck*, Ms. Shelly," they shouted. "At your service."

Then they turned their eyes to Zoë.

CHAPTER 13: HERO HURRICANE

Twelve against one! The heroes should have known. Chicken eggs always came in dozens. It was no surprise that cluck-o-bots did, too.

"Hang on, Zoë!" Andrew called to his little sister. "We're throwing it into overdrive."

"De-fense!" Abigail chanted like a fan at a football game. "De-fense!"

If Zoë could hang on for just a few seconds, the twins would arrive.

And arrive they did—in style. Abigail bowled and Andrew rolled, right over the competition. By using their superpowers together, they cut a path through the crowd from back to front. Chickens, feathers, and cluck-o-bots tumbled out of their way and into the gutter. Talk about an eight-ten split. The twins had bowled the very first egg-hen split.

The battle, however, wasn't won. It was just about to begin. Abigail and Andrew joined Zoë on the picnic table, and the cluck-o-bots surrounded them. Safely behind her robotic troops, Shelly shrieked commands.

"Scramble them!" she screeched. "Poach them! Don't go over easy!" Shelly might have been wearing an egg costume, but she really had eggs on her brain.

"Her name should be Egghead," Abigail said under her breath.

"Cock-a-doodle-downfall!" the cluck-o-bots squawked, rushing forward in a cluster like a flock of migrating birds.

Andrew reacted first. He spread his arms and urgently reached for his sisters. Tiny wheels popped out of his shoes.

"Hero Hurricane!" he shouted. "Grab my hands!"

Hero Hurricane wasn't what you might expect. It wasn't a warning or the name of a tropical storm. Hero Hurricane was a super-powered spin that only Andrew could perform.

Hand-in-hand-in-hand, the heroic trio started to twirl. Zoë led with her fists, Abigail her feet.

Punch! Kick! Clobber! Hit! The cluck-o-bots ran into a swirling storm.

Down they went, left and right. One punch or kick was all it took. Then their heads popped up on long springs like stretched-out Slinkys. None of them would be getting up soon.

"Fun!" Zoë squealed, delighted with Hero Hurricane. Who knew that clobbering cluck-o-bots could be such a thrill?

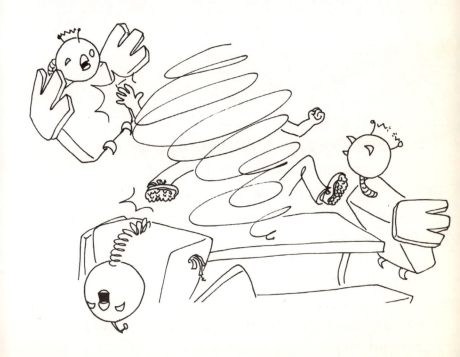

But like most thrills, this one ended too soon. One second the heroes were spinning. The next a moldy green egg landed on the picnic table and cracked open. Stinky yellow gas started to pour out of it like a smoke bomb.

"Go to sleep!" Shelly snickered, a gas mask covering her face.

The heroes had already breathed the gas. Before they could count to three, they passed out. They fell into deep sleep right there on the picnic table.

Heroes A^{2}Z had been defeated.

CHAPTER 14: EGGSITTING

"Pee-yew," Andrew muttered, slowly opening his eyes.

Nearby Abigail stirred awake. "*W*-what happened?"

"Fumes," Zoë said, and that single word explained everything. The heroes had been gassed. Shelly had put them to sleep with a rotten egg. What a stinky trick!

"But where are we now?" Andrew wondered. The last place he remembered being was at the park. This was definitely somewhere else.

The heroes were indoors. They were prisoners in an icy building Shelly called Castle Eggloo. It was part castle and part igloo. The heroes occupied a small square room with three white walls. The fourth wall was made of icy bars.

"Jail!" Abigail exclaimed. "We've been locked in a jail cell."

Which was no trouble for Zoë. Using her super strength, she grasped a bar in each hand and pulled. *Crack-snap!* The bars shattered like glass.

"Time to go on offense," Abigail said. "Let's get out of here."

Like a team captain taking the field, she led her siblings out of the cell and into an icy corridor. Across from them stood a second cell. Inside it paced a pack of forlorn foxes wearing striped prison suits.

Abigail frowned. "Only a chicken lover like Shelly would put foxes in jail," she grumbled.

Zoë and Andrew agreed. More importantly, they decided to come back later and free the foxes. Just as soon as Shelly was behind bars.

Soon the hallway opened into a large crowded room. Rows of nests filled the place like benches in a sports stadium. On every nest sat a person keeping eggs warm like an attentive mother hen.

The room, the heroes realized, was a human henhouse!

"Freaky," Zoë gasped. Before today she had heard of babysitting, housesitting, and even dogsitting. Now she could add eggsitting to that list. Not that she had ever wanted to add it.

"Cruise over here," Andrew called. He had found a low tunnel that exited the henhouse.

In fact, the tunnel exited the whole icy building. Soon the heroes stepped outside Castle Eggloo and into a long field.

But even with the sky open overhead, they felt just as trapped as they had indoors. Tall bleachers surrounded them on all sides, and in every seat sat a chicken.

A loud voice boomed over a speaker. "Let the games begin!"

CHAPTER 15: FRANKENBEAK AND HOOFENSTEIN

The voice on the speaker belonged to Shelly. She was perched on a platform across the field, shouting into an egg-shaped megaphone. Or would that make it an egg-a-phone? Knowing Shelly, it would.

"Let the games begin," she repeated. "Blow the Horn of Heroes!"

Next to her, an important-looking chicken puffed out its chest and stood up very straight. Then it raised a mighty horn to its beak and blew.

Too-too-tah-toooooo!

The thunderous blast of the Horn stunned the heroes and silenced the crowd. Whatever was about to happen, Shelly meant business.

Throom! Boom!

Two massive robots leaped from the bleachers and onto the field. The first was the biggest cluck-o-bot the heroes had ever seen. If robots could grow muscles, this one had grown them double. To give it an even tougher look, it gripped a long pointed pole like a weapon in one wing.

The second robot was an egg, or maybe a horse. No, it was both. The robot looked like a horse that had hatched halfway out of an egg. Only its head, legs, and hooves stuck out.

"Behold Michigan's new team of superheroes!" Shelly shouted into her egg-a-phone. "Tremble before Frankenbeak and his faithful steed Hoofenstein."

The pair of robots was exactly what their names suggested they would be. As brawny and muscular as Frankenstein, just less green, Frankenbeak even had bolts sticking out of his neck.

"Defend thyselves," he bellowed at the heroes in old-fashioned speech. "Or art thou cowards?"

Cowards! Zoë scowled and balled her hands into fists. No one called her chicken. Especially not a chicken.

"Fearless," she told Frankenbeak. Then to her siblings, she said, "Follow."

They did, and Zoë pointed at a rocking horse and croquet mallet sitting unused in the snow. The twins hadn't noticed them earlier. Now that they had, they weren't pleased. Because they finally understood Shelly's plan. She wanted the heroes to play chicken with Frankenbeak.

CHAPTER 16: PLAYING CHICKEN

Andrew vaulted onto the rocking horse and grabbed its reins. "I'll steer," he announced.

"Fuel," added Zoë, meaning she would push and provide the muscle.

That left the croquet mallet for Abigail. She scooped it up and took a seat behind her brother.

"We don't look much like knights in shining armor," she said glumly.

Which was what Shelly wanted. A game of chicken on horseback was like a jousting competition between knights. The heroes didn't stand a chance against Frankenbeak.

Once the heroes were ready, Shelly called for the Horn of Heroes to be blown again. Then she raised her arms, waited for silence, and shouted into her egg-a-phone.

"Do you have any last words?" she asked the heroes, and all three of them nodded.

"We sure do," Abigail replied. "Three of them. We're gonna beat you fast."

"Faster," Andrew said.

"Fastest!" Zoë cried, and then she threw her shoulder into the rocking horse.

Yee-haw! The heroes started to speed across the snowy field.

Charging fearlessly, the heroes felt like real knights. Andrew crouched low in the saddle. Abigail gripped her mallet in both fists. Zoë pushed powerfully. The world had never seen a braver trio, they thought. But the feeling didn't last long.

Frankenbeak kicked its heels and Hoofenstein took off. Unlike the heroes, the robot had been built and programmed especially for this game. Chicken, you could say, was in the rooster's blood.

Kah-bloooom!

The heroes, Frankenbeak, and Hoofenstein collided in midfield. Wood snapped, metal shrieked, and the riders flew into the air.

"Ow!" Andrew grunted, landing on his backside.

"Oof!" Abigail winced, bouncing on hers.

Yet the biggest bump came from the littlest of them. Zoë landed with a thump, and then a second thump thumped her.

"Flattened," she groaned, gasping for breath. Hoofenstein had landed square on her chest!

Frankenbeak, however, had landed on his feet. Before Abigail and Andrew could get to theirs, he strode over to them and glared down. He looked impossibly tall. In one wing, he clutched a greasy drumstick the size of a holiday ham.

"Dost thou have any more last words?" he sneered.

Then he raised his drumstick like the strongman at a country fair. In an instant it would drop like a hammer.

CHAPTER 17:
ROOSTER-GO-ROUND

"Roll!" Andrew cried, calling out for what he did best. Roll, spin, twist, and turn. He could spin like a human tornado on a tilt-a-whirl at the carnival. Mom called him a cement mixer because of the way he twisted up his blankets while sleeping at night.

Whoomp!

Frankenbeak slammed the ground with his oversized drumstick. Droplets of grease splattered on the snow. But not a single drop struck Andrew or Abigail. They rolled away just in time like snow angels on a mission.

"Stand and fight!" Frankenbeak roared. "Thou canst not run forever!"

Ha! Abigail almost laughed. Frankenbeak obviously didn't know her very well. Running was one of her specialties, just like rolling was for Andrew. Abigail might actually be able to run forever. She just hadn't tried yet.

Besides, who wanted to grow old in the same old pair of sweaty running shoes?

So Abigail took Frankenbeak's advice. She stopped running, stood, and fought. But not before reaching into her duffel bag and strapping on her boxing gloves.

"Round one!" Shelly exclaimed into her egg-a-phone. She wanted to see a fight, as long as her robot won.

Of course, that wasn't what happened. Frankenbeak wasn't boxing just anyone. He was squaring off against Abigail Triple-A, the All-American Athlete.

First she dodged and ducked, looking for an opening. Then she slammed and struck. Forget floating like a butterfly and stinging like a bee. Abigail wound up like a windmill and hit like a hammer.

WHAM!

The powerful blow sent Frankenbeak spinning around, and Andrew kept him whirling. After Abigail struck, her twin grabbed the robot by its wing and gave it a mighty twirl. As a result, Frankenbeak became the world's first rooster-go-round.

Vroo-oooom!

Needless to say, it wasn't a big hit on the playgrounds.

What was a big hit, you ask? Zoë. She could lift almost anything, even a big chunk of the Mackinaw Bridge*. So it was only a matter of time before she managed to get her hands under Hoofenstein. Then up it came, up she came, and into the air they soared.

Bonk! Right onto Frankenbeak's head. Talk about a hit. Abigail called it a game-winning home run.

"It's outta here!" she cheered.

Although into here would have been closer to the truth. Because Frankenbeak's spinning combined with the bonk on his head sent him into the ground like a drill.

*See Heroes A2Z #2: Bowling Over Halloween

"I've seen chickens sitting on eggs before," Andrew grinned. "But never an egg sitting on a chicken."

"Funny," Zoë laughed.

Funny indeed, except for one fact. Shelly wasn't laughing. She wasn't even anywhere in sight. She had quietly vanished into the crowd of countless chickens.

Shelly had escaped!

CHAPTER 18:
BARK THEN BWACK

"Where did Shelly go?" Abigail asked, turning and squinting up at the crowd. Thousands and thousands of chickens occupied the bleachers above her and her siblings. Shelly could be hiding anywhere among them.

"Too many chickens," Andrew complained. "We'll never find her."

Zoë disagreed. Better yet, she had an idea on how to clear out the chickens.

"Foxes," she said, heading back into Castle Eggloo.

Abigail caught onto her sister's plan immediately. She even beat her inside and to the cell where the foxes were being held.

"I'll get you out," she told the imprisoned animals. "Stand back."

Clutching a hockey stick in both hands, she whacked the bars of the cell. Crash! The bars crumbled like icicles.

"Cross-checking," Abigail said. "That's two minutes in the penalty box. Unless you're already there. Then you get to come out. Game on!"

The foxes barked and scampered out of the cell. They had no idea what Abigail was saying, but they knew they had been set free.

They didn't waste a moment of their freedom either. They tore out of the cell and started doing what foxes everywhere loved to do. They chased chickens. In moments they were outside Castle Eggloo and in the bleachers.

Bark! Bark! Bark! Then *bwack! Bwack! Bwack!*

The chickens panicked at the sight of the pack. They dashed right. They dashed left. They dashed right away and left. Soon the heroes were alone on the field.

All that remained in the bleachers were a few stray feathers, the Horn of Heroes, and Shelly. She scowled down at the heroes like a child who had been caught and sent to her room.

"This isn't over," she snapped. "I can rebuild my robots and brew more Fowl Mouthwash."

She meant business, too. Because in her hands she clutched two more of the gassy green eggs she had thrown at the heroes earlier. Even Abigail, Andrew, and Zoë were powerless against their foul fumes.

CHAPTER 19: HORN OF HEROES

"Hold your breath!" Abigail shouted.

"Plug your nose!" Andrew cried.

Above them, Shelly stood on the platform in the bleachers. In each hand she gripped a green egg like a grenade.

Yet for some reason, Zoë seemed unafraid. She didn't plug her nose and she didn't hold her breath. She snatched the Horn of Heroes, raised it to her lips, and blew.

Too-too-tah-toooooo!

Zoë blew the Horn of Heroes like it had never been blown before. She blew it louder, longer, and like only a superhero could. The bleachers rattled. The ground shook. Abigail and Andrew gave up plugging their noses and covered their ears instead.

Even Shelly covered her ears. That was her last mistake. Because when she did, she dropped her eggs. Plip, plop! They hit the ground, cracked, and released their sleeping gas. Shelly shrieked, but there was nothing else she could do.

Her shriek quickly turned into a snore. A snore followed by a thud followed by more snoring. Shelly was asleep on her feet, then asleep on her face. Neither position mattered to her. She would sleep for the rest of the day and night.

Luckily the heroes were far enough away from the fumes this time to stay awake. Only Shelly breathed them in and fell asleep.

Now, instead of a dangerous super villain, Shelly was just a snoozing kid. She was even wearing a pair of fuzzy pink pajamas. The blast of the Horn of Heroes had shattered her egg costume. She had been wearing PJ's underneath the costume the whole time.

"She doesn't look so scary now," said Abigail.

"Frail," Zoë agreed.

"Leave her alone!" a new voice shouted.

"She needs to rest!" cried a second.

The heroes turned to see a man and woman running out of Castle Eggloo. The couple was two of the people who had been sitting on eggs inside.

"She's our daughter," the woman explained. "She didn't mean to hurt anyone."

The man, Shelly's father, scooped Shelly carefully into his arms. "She has a fever," he said. "We need to get her home to bed."

Just like that, the danger was past. Shelly was asleep and in her parents' care. The crazy chickens had fled, and the people of Frankencoop were slowly remembering that they really lived in Frankenmuth.

"What was that noise?" asked a man in a suit who had wandered out of Castle Eggloo.

"I heard it, too," said a little girl. "Is it time to wake up?"

"It was the Horn of Heroes," Abigail said, the first to realize what had happened. "Hearing it cured the townsfolk of their chicken fever. They don't think they're chickens anymore."

Zoë nodded and streaked into the sky. She flew from Frankenmuth to Fruitport and from Farmington to Flint. At every stop she blew the Horn of Heroes and the people nearby stopped acting like chickens.

Her last stop was in Fowlerville. She found the chickens that had fled Frankenmuth there.

"Free," she told them. Never again would heroes and chickens be enemies.

Unfortunately the heroes still had plenty of enemies. Some could look as harmless and cute as the Easter Bunny. Some could burst from fudge shops on Halloween. One could even be as cool and famous as a …

Book #7:
Guitar Rocket Star

www.realheroesread.com

Visit the Website

realheroesread.com

Meet Authors Charlie & David
Read Sample Chapters
See Fan Artwork
Join the Free Fan Club
Invite Charlie & David to Your School
Lots More!

Real Heroes Read!

#1: Alien Ice Cream
#2: Bowling Over Halloween
#3: Cherry Bomb Squad
#4: Digging For Dinos
#5: Easter Egg Haunt
#6: Fowl Mouthwash
#7: Guitar Rocket Star

... and more!

Visit
www.realheroesread.com
for the latest news

Also by David Anthony and Charles David

Knightscares

Monsters. Magic. Mystery.

#1: Cauldron Cooker's Night
#2: Skull in the Birdcage
#3: Early Winter's Orb
#4: Voyage to Silvermight
#5: Trek Through Tangleroot
#6: Hunt for Hollowdeep
#7: The Ninespire Experiment
#8: Aware of the Wolf

Visit
www.realheroesread.com
to learn more

#1: Cauldron Cooker's Night

#2: Skull in the Birdcage

#3: Early Winter's Orb

#4: Voyage to Silvermight
The Dragonsbane Horn Book One

#5: Trek Through Tangleroot
The Dragonsbane Horn Book Two

#6: Hunt for Hollowdeep
The Dragonsbane Horn Book Three

#7: The Ninespire Experiment

#8: Aware of the Wolf

ABIGAIL

TRIPLE A
ALL AMERICAN ATHLETE

ZOË

ZUPER ZOË

Like Our Superheroes?
Let's See Yours!

DRAWING CONTEST!

Draw anything you like. Superheroes, animals, monsters, castles, or your favorite pet rock. We don't care what you draw. Just send your drawings along with your name and address to:

Real Heroes Read!
P.O. Box 654
Union Lake, MI 48387

Your drawing could appear on the realheroesread.com website or in an upcoming Heroes A2Z book!

Get Drawing. You could be famous!

Want to Order Your Very Own Autographed Heroes A2Z or Knightscares Book?

Here's How:

(1) Check the books you want on the next page.
(2) Fill out the address information at the bottom.
(3) Add up the total price for the books you want.

Heroes A2Z cost $4.99 each.
Knightscares cost $5.99 each.

(4) Add $1.00 shipping per book.
(5) Michigan residents include 6% sales tax.
(6) Send check or money order along with the next page to:

Real Heroes Read!
P.O. Box 654
Union Lake, MI 48387

Thank You!

Please allow 3-4 weeks for shipping

- [ ] Heroes A2Z #1: Alien Ice Cream
- [ ] Heroes A2Z #2: Bowling Over Halloween
- [ ] Heroes A2Z #3: Cherry Bomb Squad
- [ ] Heroes A2Z #4: Digging For Dinos
- [ ] Heroes A2Z #5: Easter Egg Haunt
- [ ] Heroes A2Z #6: Fowl Mouthwash
- [ ] Knightscares #1: Cauldron Cooker's Night
- [ ] Knightscares #2: Skull in the Birdcage
- [ ] Knightscares #3: Early Winter's Orb
- [ ] Knightscares #4: Voyage to Silvermight
- [ ] Knightscares #5: Trek Through Tangleroot
- [ ] Knightscares #6: Hunt for Hollowdeep
- [ ] Knightscares #7: The Ninespire Experiment
- [ ] Knightscares #8: Aware of the Wolf

Total $ Enclosed: _____

Autograph To: _____
Name: _____
Address: _____
City, State, Zip: _____

About the Illustrator
Lys Blakeslee

Lys graduated from Grand Valley State University in Michigan where she earned a degree in Illustration.

She has always loved to read, and devoted much of her childhood to devouring piles of books from the library.

She lives in Wyoming, MI with her wonderful parents, two goofy cats, and one extra-loud parakeet.

Her preferred way to eat eggs is scrambled, with deviled eggs a close second.

Thank you, Lys!